Witch's Apprentice
And
Argon's Labyrinth

Witch's Apprentice and Argon's Labyrinth

Kathryn Leo

Copyright © 2022 Kathryn Leo.

All rights reserved. No part of this book may be reproduced in any form or by any electronic or mechanical means, including information storage and retrieval systems, without permission in writing from the publisher, except by reviewers, who may quote brief passages in a review.

ISBN: 978-1-959434-13-9 (Paperback Edition)
ISBN: 978-1-959434-14-6 (Hardcover Edition)
ISBN: 978-1-959434-12-2 (E-book Edition)

Some characters and events in this book are fictitious. Any similarity to the real persons, living or dead, is coincidental and not intended by the author.

Book Ordering Information

The Regency Publishers, US
521 5th Ave 17th floor NY, NY10175
Phone Number: (315)537-3088 ext 1007
Email: info@theregencypublishers.com
www.theregencypublishers.com

Printed in the United States of America

CONTENTS

Chapter 1 1
Chapter 2 4
Chapter 3 8
Chapter 4 10
Chapter 5 12
Chapter 6 14
Chapter 7 17
Chapter 8 20
Chapter 9 22
Chapter 10 24
Chapter 11 26
Chapter 12 28
Chapter 13 31
Chapter 14 32
Chapter 15 34
Chapter 16 36
Chapter 17 38
Chapter 18 40
Chapter 19 42
Chapter 20 44
Chapter 21 46

CHAPTER 1

It was a familiar sound of a bird squawking that stopped me from picking wild berries in the Black Forest. It was the sound of an omen bird that sat on the berry bush. This wasn't the first time I saw an omen bird. I once saw an omen bird in the Black Forest when I was young. I was lost in the forest, and I saw the bird before finding my way out. An omen bird is a sign when something magical like an elf, a warlock, or a witch is close by. I wasn't afraid of the bird because I believed that something magical found me and guided me back home when I was lost.

"Beth!" cried a voice from a distance. The bird flew away. I turned around and saw farmer Tom walking toward me.

"Hi, Tom," I said.

"I wanted to let you know there will be a meeting at the village hall at three. I was hoping you can make it," said Tom.

"I'll be there," I replied.

When I arrived back at my house, I saw mother cleaning the house as she liked to do repetitively. "Mother! You should be in bed," I said.

"I'm feeling well today, and the house needs a good clean," she replied.

"You're still look sick, and I picked some wild berries to make you better."

"Oh, Beth! You know you shouldn't be wandering around in the Black Forest. You'll get lost again."

"I was ten. I'm older now."

I placed some berries into a bowl and handed it to Mother. "I'm going to a meeting this afternoon. We have to prepare for winter. I'll ask the council if we can get warmer blankets," I said.

"Okay, dear," she replied.

I headed upstairs to the bathroom and ran a hot bath. I allowed the hot water to ease away all my tension and all my worries. I bathed for a good ten minutes before getting out. After drying myself, I wrapped the towel around me and headed down the hall to my bedroom. I got changed into something warm and clean then brushed my knotted long blond hair. I looked at the clock on the wall and saw that it was twenty to three.

I arrived at the town hall, a large sandstone building that was old but in good condition. I walked inside and was overpowered by the smell of body odour and the heat that came from a room full of farmers, labourers, and professions that make up the people of Sandsdale.

"The drought has killed half of our crops. There's not enough food produced from the farms to make it through to winter," said Tom to the council.

"We will have to rely heavily on the king's rations," said Peter Sims, who was the head spokesman of the council.

"The king will only offer flour and rice. We need meat and vegetables. People are hungry and many are sick and need medicine," Tom replied.

"We need a solution!" said one of the labourers.

"What about getting help from a witch?" said a lady standing behind me. I turned around and saw an attractive lady with pale white skin, long black hair, and green eyes.

"Did you say get help from a witch?" questioned Peter. "Who are you, lady? What is your name?"

"I am Zelda, a witch." Everyone in the room fell silent. "What do you want, witch?" asked another member of the council.

"I am looking for someone to train as a witch," she replied. "To train as a witch?" questioned Peter. "What for?"

"To work for me. He or she needs to learn magic before working in the witches' village to make materials to trade with the king."

"A witch's apprentice?" said Peter.

"Yes! I want someone here to become a witch, and in return, I will lift the drought and hasten your crops to grow."

"There will be no magic here," said Peter loudly. "Besides, it's forbidden for a human to become a witch. His or her soul would be damned."

"No, it won't!" cried Zelda.

"I'll do it," I said. Everyone in the room looked at me. "No, you won't, young girl," said Tom.

"Please, Tom," I begged. "My mother is sick. The king does little to help us, and we all need help."

"But your mother needs you," said Tom.

"My mother needs me to make a deal with the witch," I beg again.

"What is your name, young girl?" asked the witch. "Bethany Hardings. People call me Beth."

"Well, Beth, I am happy to train you as a witch." "No!" said Peter.

"Please," I begged for a third time.

Peter said, "I will ask everyone here to put their hand up if Beth should go with the witch." Most of the people in the room raised their hands. "Okay, you can go with the witch," replied Peter, "but be warned that witches are not trustworthy and your soul is in jeopardy."

"I will be fine," I replied. *I cannot believe I'm going to be a witch*, I think to myself. I know everyone in Sandsdale think witches are untrustworthy, but I am sure it was a witch that was looking out for me when I got lost in the forest, and I trust them with my life.

Zelda took out a wand from her handbag, waved it around, and chanted, "As we go, lift the sorrow so the plants may grow." She then tapped the wand on my wrist and a silver metal band appeared. "This band is magical. You cannot run away from me while the band is on you. Try to escape and you will only come back to me."

"I need to say goodbye to my mother." I ran and told my mother the news. She was upset. I promised her that I would return soon. I then packed my bags and left the house. Zelda was waiting in a closed cart, which was pulled by a beautiful black stallion. I entered the cart, and we left heading north into the Black Forest.

It took five hours before we arrived at the witches' village. It was rather large and everything seemed tidy and new. We stopped in front of a small wooden cottage with its exterior painted purple.

"This is your new home," said Zelda. "It may not look much on the outside but on the inside it looks like a palace."

"It looks welcoming to me," I replied. "Well, well, I thought the cat had got your tongue. This is the first time you've said anything since we left. You need to speak while you are staying with me. I won't tolerate a mute girl."

I realized that Zelda had been telling the truth when I entered the cottage. There were many rooms and all the rooms were large and beautifully decorated.

"You must be hungry. You will find salad sandwiches in the fridge in the kitchen," said Zelda. She showed me to the kitchen and opened a large fridge and saw several wrapped sandwiches. Next to the sandwiches, I saw a bowl of dried cockroaches and marinated slugs.

"Ooo, yuck!" I cried.

"Oh yes! Bethany, witches love foods that humans find gross, and we find gross that humans eat like chicken or pork meat." I took a salad sandwich and ate it rather hastily. "Slow down," she said. As soon as my belly was full, I gave a big yawn. I was then taken upstairs to a large bedroom. It had a large bed, bigger than a king-sized bed.

"This will be your bedroom," Zelda said. "You will find spare pyjamas and clothes in the cupboard if you haven't packed enough. Sleep now. I will explain what is expected of you tomorrow."

CHAPTER 2

I found myself waking up lying on the corner of the bed. I didn't know what time it was for there were no clocks on the wall, all I knew was that the sun was up and it was a bright day. I opened the door and walked down a long corridor. After opening five doors, I finally found the bathroom. It took me a while to prepare for the morning as I was still weary from yesterday's journey. I felt better after showering and changing into something comfortable. I went downstairs and saw Zelda making breakfast in the kitchen, and I noticed a clock in the kitchen that read 7:15.

"Hi, my dear. I'm making some porridge for you," said Zelda. I took a seat at the kitchen table feeling hungry that I could eat anything. I ate the porridge with pleasure and felt instantly full.

"Thank you, Zelda," I said. She then took out what appeared to be orange juice out of the fridge. "Yum, I love orange juice," I said.

"It's not orange juice, my dear. It's a potion. It will give you the potential to cast spells." She poured me a cup. I hesitantly sipped it and found that it tasted like orange juice. "Now you won't be able to cast spells right away. You will need to be trained first. I will teach you some spells today then tomorrow you will be trained at a witch school."

"How long will the training take?" I said.

"It should take you a year if you're good," Zelda replied. I felt melancholy at the thought of going to a witch school. "When you finish school, you will use your magic to make special garments and supplies for the king's army."

"Why me?" I asked.

"Young witches and even humans training to be witches can work smaller jobs faster."

"How long will this take?" I asked.

"A year at school and another year to work." I felt my mood darken. Two years was a long time to be away from home, and Mum needed me. "You will start school tomorrow. For today, I will give you a wand, and I will show you some simple spells." After breakfast, she showed me how to clean the house using magic. It took me half a day to get it, but when I waved the wand around and focused, the broom started to sweep the floor, the rags began to wipe the bench, and the vacuum cleaner began to vacuum the carpet. It was my moment of glory when the house was spotless at the end of the day. "Mother would be happy with this spell," I said to Zelda.

The next day, Zelda woke me up from a deep sleep. It was still dark, and it was much too early to get out of bed. "What time is it?" I said.

"Time for you to go to school," Zelda replied.

After getting ready, we headed off to school by horse and cart. After an hour of travelling, we stopped in front of the school building, which looked like a castle. Waiting for us was an old man with a long grey beard and long hair tied back in a ponytail. "I want you to meet the headmaster of the school," said Zelda.

"Well hello, Zelda. Who is this sweet angel with you?" he asked.

"My name is Bethany Hardings. People call me Beth," I said.

"My name is Maxalon. I am the headmaster, and I will be taking you to class," he said. After climbing five sets of stairs, we stopped in front of a large blue door. Maxalon gave a loud knock and an elderly lady with a crooked nose and glasses opened the door.

"I am your teacher, Miss Winton," she said.

I refrained myself from laughing out loud. She was the type of witch I read of in fairy tales. "My name is Bethany Hardings, ma'am. People call me Beth."

I was shown inside and saw a room full of young witches staring at me with their green eyes. Green was the colour of all witches' eyes.

My eyes were blue, so I stood out and everyone could tell that I was human. I looked around the room and saw one spare seat. I sat next to a girl with short brown hair and olive skin. "Hi," I said to her, but she did not speak.

"I would like to start our topic today on different types of witches," said Miss Winton. "First of all, there is what we call a white witch. These witches harness magic for good purposes. Everyone here is a white witch, and you will use your magic to do good things. The other type is a black witch and, as you probably guess, use magic for evil purposes. Using magic for evil purposes is against the law and can offer life imprisonment. There are witches that do controversial spells, these are called grey witches. It is not illegal, but you could be ostracized by other witches." With this knowledge, I looked at my band and wondered what type Zelda was.

After listening to a half a day's lecture, I heard the bell ring. Miss Winton said it was the lunch bell, and we had an hour for lunch before returning back to her class for our first practical lesson. I didn't know my way around school, so I followed all the students and ended up at the school's cafeteria. I looked at the menu and saw that they had a selection of fried bat's wings, cicadas, roasted slug, and tomato soup. I felt disgusted at the thought of eating all but one, so I chose the tomato soup. After ordering the soup, I found a spare table and sat on my own. I looked around me and noticed that a group of witches at the table next to me were staring.

"They're just curious about you," said a voice behind me. I turned around and saw a handsome, athletic-looking wizard with long brown hair and a cute smile. I blushed.

"Um...er, sorry," I said.

"Don't be afraid of making friends with witches. We are all friendly," he said.

"Oh," I replied, still a little speechless. "My name is Zanda."

"Hi, Zanda. My name is Beth," I said. "Can I sit with you?"

"Yeah, sure," I replied.

"So what brings you to Desmand College?"

"I'm training to be a witch. I've made a deal with a witch," I said.

"Oh, what kind of deal?" he said curiously.

"I come from a village called Sandsdale. We rely on our farms for fresh food but half our crops died due to the drought. I've made a deal with a witch to end the drought and to make the plants grow quickly. In return, I learn and work for her."

"Why don't you ask the king for help?" he asked. "The king doesn't give us enough food to eat."

"Oh, that's terrible," he replied. "It's not the king's fault. There is a powerful warlock controlling the king. He is wicked." "What's a warlock?" I asked. "A warlock is like a powerful witch, but their power comes more naturally. Witches need training, and our power comes in different categories. There are three categories: castor one, castor two, and castor three witches. Everyone will graduate here being a castor one witch. Older witches around forty and older are castor two witches. Their power is stronger. The most powerful witches are castor three. Any witch with a gift can be a castor three. Most witches use green magic but special witches have blue magic. With this magic, they can be very powerful."

"More powerful than the warlock?" I asked. "About the same," he replied.

"Are there any castor three witches?" I questioned.

"There a no known castor three witches around, but it's been prophesied that we will have one soon."

"Well, I hope so," I said.

"So who are you working for?" he asked.

"Her name is Zelda," I replied.

"I know Zelda. She's a controversial witch."

"Is she a black witch? I've been learning about them," I said.

"No. I know she could be classified as a grey witch, but she's had a hard life and everyone looks the other way."

"Hard life?" I replied.

"Yes, it was prophesied that she would have a child who would grow up to be the most powerful witch of all. One day, the warlock paid her a visit and cast a powerful spell to prevent her having children."

"Oh, that's awful!" I said.

"Yeah, she turned forty last year, and now she's a castor two. She's becoming more controversial, getting away with darker spells to meet her own needs."

I heard the bell ring, and it was time to go back to class. I said goodbye to Zanda and promised that we would meet again the same time tomorrow. I made my way back to Miss Winton's class and sat next to the same girl with olive skin.

"Let us start the class today casting a spell to make a flower grow in one minute," said Miss Winton. She gave us all a pot and seeds. "Now plant the seed, wave your wand, and chant 'With the seeds I sow, it's time to grow.'"

I planted the seeds and chanted the spell. Nothing happened. I did it again and again but nothing happened. The olive-skinned girl looked at me and laughed. I had to focus. I closed my eyes, took a deep breath, and waved my wand around. "With the seeds I sow, it's time to grow," I chanted. I suddenly saw the seeds sprout.

"Well done!" said the olive-skinned girl. "Thanks," I replied.

"Sorry to laugh at you before. I didn't think you were going to do it."

"That's okay. I didn't think I was going to do it either." "My name is Daisy," she said with a glow on her cheeks. "My name is Beth," I replied.

"I would be delighted if we could be friends," she said. "I would love to be your friend."

It was five o'clock when I arrived back at Zelda's. I found her asleep on the couch in the lounge room. I crept my way to the kitchen, hoping to find something to eat. I found a note saying, "Please help yourself to the snail salad in the fridge." Despite the disgusting thought of having snails in my salad, I plucked out the snails and ate the lettuce, tomato, and olives. After my meal, I gave a big yawn and headed for the bedroom to prepare for bed.

The next day in class, Miss Winton showed us colour spells. We spent all morning turning things into different colours for no purpose but to have a bit of fun with magic. Miss Winton said having fun is important to becoming a good witch. Daisy turned my hair to blue, red, purple, and back to blonde. I turned Daisy's skin into bronze then laughed saying that she looked like a statue. After we were done, Miss Winton assembled us back together again and said that after lunch that we have to meet at the sports ground, and Mr. Huxley would teach us self-defence every Tuesday afternoon.

Miss Winton gave us an hour lecture on how witches are vulnerable and need self-defence to overcome our threats. It was twelve o'clock when the lunch bell rang.

"Oh good. I'm hungry," said Daisy, rubbing her tummy. "Oh, Daisy, come hang out with me and Zanda," I begged. "Oooh. who's Zanda?" she teased.

"We are just friends," I explained.

"No. I want to leave you two alone. My witch's instincts are telling me that he likes you, and he's going to ask you out." My face went red wondering how she could possibly know this.

I walked alone to the cafeteria and saw Zanda sitting at the same place we met yesterday. He was chewing on some bat wings that didn't seem at all appetizing.

"Hey, how are you?" I said.

"Good. Try some bat wings. It tastes great."

"No thanks," I said, scrunching up my nose. I went to the cafeteria and ordered pumpkin soup. We sat and ate our meals and talked about our morning.

"Hey, I was wondering." Zanda spoke in a nervous voice. "Yes?" I said.

"I won't be here tomorrow because I work at the stables Wednesday till Saturdays. I thought it would be nice if I can show you around on Saturday when you're not attending school."

"I would be delighted," I replied.

It seemed like we barely talked when it was time to go back to class. Zanda showed me to the sports ground, and I met up with the class for self-defence.

"Okay, class. It's time we start our first lesson in self-defence. We are going to learn how to disappear to hide from the enemy," said Mr. Huxley.

"This sounds fun. I can use this to hide from my annoying aunt when she comes around," said Daisy.

"This is going to be a silent spell so your enemies can't hear you. I want you to wave your wand around once and think about being invisible to your enemy."

I took out my wand and thought about hiding from everyone around me. It worked on the first go.

CHAPTER 3

It was a Saturday morning, and I was excited to meet Zanda. Zelda knocked on the door and walked in the room. "It's time for you to get ready, Beth, and remember our agreement. If you find yourself behind in class, you cannot see Zanda anymore. I think boys will distract you from important things, and you are better off without them."

"Oh, I won't fall behind. I promise!" I jumped out of bed, quickly had a shower, and changed into an old cotton top and denim jeans. Zelda made me toast and orange juice for breakfast. After breakfast, there was a knock on the door. I opened the door, and Zanda was standing there with flowers in his hand.

"Oh, Zanda, they're beautiful!" I said. I took the flowers and placed them in an empty glass vase that was on the kitchen table.

"I have a cart waiting for you to go to the stables. It's about an hour trip," Zanda said. We entered the cart and the horse took off without anyone to guide him except the use of magic to lead him to our destination.

"Oh, Zanda. I can't wait to see all the horses. It will be my pleasure feeding them."

"That's great," he replied. "But first, there is someone I would like you to meet."

We arrived at the stables an hour later. We walked past half a dozen stables without meeting any of the horses. We arrived at a large stable and entered. I heard a neigh of a horse behind large doors. Zanda took out keys from his pocket and unlocked the door and opened it. "Come on. Don't be shy. I want you to meet someone," said Zanda to the horse.

I saw the head of a beautiful white horse. He came trotting out, and I saw that he had wings. "It's a Pegasus!" I shouted.

"That's right, and I want to take him out and fly him," replied Zanda.

"Oh, Zanda! Can we? What's his name?" "His name is Snow," he replied.

It didn't take long to prepare Snow for a flight. My head was spinning at the thought of riding a Pegasus. I've never seen one before, but it is often talked about in tales at home.

"Let's go," said Zanda. We went outside on to an open paddock and hopped onto the saddle.

I sat behind Zanda, holding on to him tight. Snow started to gallop then stretched his big wings out and started to fly. "Where are we going?" I said to Zanda.

"It's a surprise!" he replied.

At first I was nervous at flying, but when I saw the hills from above, I relaxed and enjoyed the scenery. It was only minutes of flying that I saw that we were approaching the Black Forest. I realized then that we were heading for my home.

"We are going to my home!" I cried.

"Yes, we are going to stop for lunch on the southerly hills of Sandsdale, and you can watch your home village from a distance."

"Oh, thank you," I replied. "I miss home."

As we flew on, I watched the Black Forest covered in a winter's mist, which gave the trees a purple hue. It didn't seem long when I saw the village of Sandsdale. "I can see the ploughs working and the crops growing," I said, and I knew everything was all right.

"We are almost there. Hold on."

I held on tight as we approached the hills. I felt nervous about landing but felt safe holding on to Zanda. As we stopped, I let go of him, and he dismounted and then helped me off. I looked over to the north and watched my home town.

"We should eat," he said. "I packed salad sandwiches."

Salad sandwiches, I thought. I was glad it wasn't bug or toad sandwiches.

After lunch, we sat down on a hillside. It was cold, and Zanda wrapped a blanket around me. He sat next to me and wrapped an arm around me. "I like you very much, Beth," he said.

"I like you too, Zanda," I replied.

"I would like to know if you would like to be my girlfriend."

I turned toward him and gave him a hug. "I would love to be your girlfriend!" I shouted as if I wanted the people of Sandsdale to hear me."

He leaned toward me and gave me a kiss on the lips. I felt a tingling sensation on my mouth.

"What was that tingling feeling?" I said.

"It happens when you kiss a witch who is in love." "You love me?" I asked.

"Yes, I do."

CHAPTER 4

"You are lit up like a Christmas tree, Beth," said Daisy. "Zanda asked me out, and I have fallen in love." "Oh, Bethany, that's wonderful."

"Okay, class, listen up. I need your attention," interrupted Miss Winton. "Today is a very important day," she continued. "Today we will test your magic's potential. The school is in search of all the potential caster threes, and I want you to find out what colour magic you have. I will give you all a bowl filled with special powder. This powder is flammable, and I want all of you to cast a fire with the powder. Most of you will light a green flame but those with the caster three potential will cast a blue flame."

All of a sudden, I felt from being on top of the world to nervous.

"Don't worry. Just relax, Beth," said Daisy.

"Okay," said Miss Winton. "I want you to really focus and get out your wand and tap the bowl three times then chant. 'This spell I cast is something special. It will tell me my potential.'"

With this instruction, we all took out our wands. "And remember that the flame will tell you your potential. You are not anything yet until you complete your training. If any of you produce a blue flame, you will be moved to a special class with all the other potential castor threes for further training and testing."

I picked up my wand and tapped the bowl three times and chanted, "This spell I cast is something special. It will tell me my potential." At first nothing happened, then smoke came up from the bowl but no flame. "It will take a while for the flame to form. Each of your flames will form at different times," explained Miss Winton.

I looked around me and saw green flames appearing in most of the bowl from the students around me. Then I saw that Daisy had a blue colour, and she shrieked.

"Congratulations, Daisy," I whispered. "Mine's taking its time." Moments later, the flame had formed, and it was blue.

I could hardly believe it. I had the potential to be a very powerful witch. What would Zelda think now?

"Congratulations, both Daisy and Bethany, you now proceed to room 1. Just go out the door, turn left, and it's at the end of the building."

We both thanked Miss Winton and headed to the classroom. I knocked on the door to room one and Maxalon open the door. "Welcome, Beth and Daisy. Allow me to introduce you to the others."

We walked in the room and saw the teacher accompanied by one girl and two boys. "I would like to first introduce you to the teacher, Mr. Flick. Mr. Flick, this is Daisy and Bethany."

"How do you do?" he spoke.

"I am well," Daisy and I spoke at once.

"Next, I would like you to meet the other students, Sampson, Jade, and Ruby." We all exchanged greetings, and I sat next to Ruby and Daisy sat next to me.

"Okay, class, listen up," said Mr. Flick. "All you are potential caster threes, and now we will start our training and testing to see who will be the most powerful witch of all witches." I heard a door shut, turned around, and noticed that Maxalon had left the room.

"Okay, pay attention," continued Mr. Flick. "I want to tell you first about the four elements of the universe. They are earth, fire, water, and air. These are the four elements a witch has to master to become a powerful witch. You will all be trained on how to master each one and you will be tested." Everyone looked at one another confused. "For example, for fire you will be learning how to extinguish the golden flame, which is the hardest to put out. And at the end of the week, you will be taken to a dragon's lair who breathes out the golden flame. You must extinguish his flame using your blue magic." Jade put his hand up. "Yes, Jade?" said Mr. Flick.

"It sounds dangerous. Will we get hurt if we don't?"

"No. The challenges you face may sound dangerous, but you will have a safety spell placed on you so you won't get hurt. We will start tomorrow with fire, then water, then earth, and then air. I will tell you each of the challenges after you pass each test."

Ruby put her hand up. "What happens when we pass all the tests? I mean, will that be it?"

"If you pass the test, you will then fight the warlock and whoever wins will become the most powerful."

"Fight the warlock?" I questioned.

"Don't worry, it's not dangerous. You will go to the Black Forest where the warlock is hiding. You will wander the forest, and whilst you're wandering the forest looking for the warlock, your reflexes will be tested."

"Reflexes? How?" I asked.

"While you're walking through the forest, mirages of the warlock will appear and will strike a beam. If this beam hits you, it will diminish your power, so I want you to you use your magic to deflect the beam. When you find the warlock, I want you to use your power to try and trap him in a special force field, where if trapped, he will lose his power. Let me tell you now, he is powerful and he will resist. Using his silver magic, he will put you in a force field and you will most likely lose."

Everyone fell silent and then I put my hand up. "Yes, Beth." "What if more than one could be a castor three?"

"No, Beth. In the natural order of things, only one, if any, can be a castor three. Anyone else with questions?"

No one moved, only silence.

"Well, if that is all, we will start tomorrow."

CHAPTER 5

I noticed everyone was staring at us when I gave Zanda a big hug.
"Pay no attention to them. What do they know about our love?" "Oh, I don't care. I'm so happy today," I replied.
"Oh yeah? What's going on?" he said.
"Well, I just found out I have blue magic, and tomorrow, I will start my training to find out how powerful I am."
He gave me a hug. "That's wonderful!" he said with a distant look on his face.
"What's the matter?" I replied.
"You could be the most powerful witch, and with that, you could live in the castle away from me."
"I will take you with me. And besides, I just want to go home and bring you with me."
"I just hope they will accept us," he said.
"They will. Well, I've got to go back to Zelda's. I need to do some study before the big day tomorrow."
"Okay. I will see you tomorrow."
I left school, and because Zelda wasn't expecting me home, I borrowed one of the school's horse and cart to get me home.
I arrived at Zelda's at 2:00 p.m., and she was out. I made myself a salad sandwich and then went to my room to study. I opened up the text that talked about different colours of magic—blue, green, silver, gold, and pink.
"Pink magic?" I said to myself and read on. "Pink magic is very powerful magic used by warlocks that can kill anyone. It is very hard to block when attacked."
As soon as I finished reading about the different colours of magic, I felt tired and laid down on the bed and drifted off to sleep. Suddenly, I found myself in the Black Forest. I was lost in the forest, and I was scared. I noticed that there was a pack of wolves watching me, and I started to run. I ran and ran for what seemed like eternity. I then tripped on a rock and fell to the ground. The wolves began to surround me and I screamed. The next thing I heard was a voice saying to wake up. I opened my eyes and saw Zelda standing next to me.
"Oh, Zelda, I had a nightmare."
"Well, it's all over now," she replied. "What are you doing home at this time?" she questioned.
"Oh, Zelda, I have good news," I said. "I have the potential to be a castor three."
"A powerful witch... you. Impossible." "Why is it impossible? I have blue magic?"
Zelda shook her head and sighed. "Let me tell you a secret. You need to pass all the tests to become a powerful witch. And for a human to become a witch, you need to take three magic potions."
"Magic potions? Why is that impossible?" I asked.

"You need to obtain three magic ingredients, and you need to go through three quests to get these ingredients. And let me tell you, these quests are impossible to complete."

"What are the quests?" I asked.

"Well, first you get the rubies from trolls. They are located in the marshlands, and it is a dangerous journey. You also have to ask permission to have some. You can't just take it, and they don't give it away to anyone. Next, you have to get a magic egg from the red phoenix. You have to convince her to lay one for you, and she hasn't shared her egg to anyone. Next, you have to obtain a magic pearl from the giant oyster, and he's stubborn as anything to give his pearl."

"Oh please!" I begged. "We have to try." "Why should I help you?" she said.

"Because I believe I can defeat the warlock, and I think that is what you want most of all," I replied with confidence, knowing that is what she wanted. Zelda sat down on the bed to think. "Please, Zelda. We must try."

"Okay then, but we must go tonight to visit the marshlands. The rubies will help you get through the first part of your testing."

"Oh, thank you, Zelda," I cried.

CHAPTER 6

We headed for the marshlands on our magic brooms. We were slow getting there, but after four hours of night flying, we arrived at the threshold of the marshlands. It was dark and misty, and I was afraid.

"This is far as we go. We cannot use our magic from this point," said Zelda. She pulled out a small sword from the end of her broom. "We have to walk the rest of the way, and things may attack us so we can defend ourselves with this."

"How long until we get there?" I said.

"An hour on foot. It will be a hard walk in the deep mud," she said. We walked onward north, and I couldn't see far in the dark with the mist blocking out the light. We didn't follow any track. There was only a deep muddy ground that acted as weights on my feet. We only walked for twenty minutes before we took our first break and stopped for a drink of water and a salad sandwich that Zelda packed. I had finished eating when we heard footsteps in the background. Zelda picked up the sword and said, "Who's there?"

I looked around and couldn't see anything and then I felt something jump on me and fell onto the muddy ground. It was a wild boar, and it was charging at me so I pushed it away. Zelda stabbed the boar and it died. I pushed the boar off me and was saturated in blood and mud.

"Come on. Let's get moving. It's not safe to stop," said Zelda. We walked on. The farther and farther we walked, the deeper and thicker the mud got. After a while, my legs began to hurt and my body began to ache. I completely relied on Zelda getting us there because there were no signs or indications on where we were.

"I hope we are not lost," I said to Zelda.

"No, we are right on track," she replied. We walked on for another twenty minutes, and after that, I felt I had to stop and rest.

"I need a break," I said.

"We will rest for a water break but only for a few minutes," replied Zelda. We stopped and I sat and melted into the thick mud. "I have a remedy to fix your weary body and give you more energy. It's a natural remedy, not a magic potion," said Zelda. Zelda presented a green cocktail in a small flask and I drank it. After a while, I felt better. "Let's go. We have to get moving," said Zelda. We walked on and it was easier.

"Apart from the boar, there has been no creatures around to attack us. This is very unusual," said Zelda.

"Thank goodness," I replied.

Suddenly, I felt a sharp sting on my leg. "Ouch!" I screamed, grasping my leg. "Something bit me." Zelda and I looked around to see what bit me but couldn't see anything.

"It could be anything, but it looks too small a bite mark to be anything dangerous. Let's get moving."

We started to walk and then I noticed eyes of some creatures staring at me. The eyes moved closer and saw then I was surrounded by wolves like in my dream. "Wolves!" I screamed.

Zelda looked around. "I can't see anything," she said.

I fell to the ground and the wolves moved in closer. I started to scream for help. Then they started to charge at me and disap- peared before they hit. More wolves appeared and started to charge at me, and I screamed some more. I put my hand over my eyes and screamed, "Please stop!" I then felt a sharp sting in my leg. My hands pulled away from my eyes and saw that the wolves were gone. I noticed Zelda had a syringe in her hand.

"You were hallucinating, Beth, so I injected you with an antihallucination remedy I have. It's another natural remedy that works against all the hallucinogenic insect that are around. You were bitten by one of them."

I felt relieved and anxious at the same time. "Thank you, Zelda. I thought I was being attacked by wolves."

"Let's go. We are almost there." We kept walking. The ten- minute walk seem an hour, and I am sure time is slow in the marshlands. All of a sudden, I couldn't move. I was stuck in mud waist-deep.

"I'm stuck, Zelda!" I cried.

"I will pull you out," she replied. Zelda grabbed my arms and pulled, but it was no use. She tried again and again, but I was still stuck. "Let's call for help. The trolls are nearby. and they are big and strong."

"Help!" we both cried. All of a sudden, we heard something pounding on the ground.

The pounding got louder, and I could make out a large figure in the distance. He looked like a tall, rounded, muscular man with green skin. "That's a troll," said Zelda. "They are very strong. They will pull you out."

The troll came close and said, "What are you two doing here?"

"We are on our way to see the leader of the trolls, but my friend here is stuck. Can you please help us?"

"I will help your friend, but you must go home." The troll picked me up and placed me on shallow ground. "There you go. I pulled you out. Now go home."

"Please, troll, we are after some rubies to make a magic potion," said Zelda.

"Ha ha ha!" The troll laughed. "We don't give away our rubies to anyone, let alone witches," he said.

"My friend here is a human training to be a witch. She has the potential to defeat the warlock with the help of your special rubies."

"Defeat the warlock?" questioned the troll. "Come with me. The leader will want to talk to you."

Zelda and I looked at each other, puzzled, and started to follow the troll. He took us to a large cave where a dozen trolls were sitting around.

"Leader! I have news for you," the troll said to another troll with blue markings all over his face. It was the leader troll.

"What is it?" he said.

"There's a couple of witches here to see you. They want some of our rubies to defeat the warlock." The leader troll laughed.

"Oh, please, sir," I said. "I am the one to challenge the warlock."

"And what makes you so sure you can do this?" he said. "I don't know. I just believe I can."

"Belief is not enough for my rubies," cried the leader troll. "I heard that the warlock is causing you problems. So it is in your interest to let her try," interrupted Zelda.

The leader troll sighed. "A few weeks ago, the warlock came here and took most of our gems for his magic potions, and he scared of most of the animals. We hunt the animals, and now food is in short supply." He thought for a moment. "If you can defeat the warlock, the animals will come back," said the leader.

"That's right," said Zelda.

"The warlock has placed a spell over the marshlands. The spell will be broken when he is defeated." The troll got up and walked over to a treasure chest. He opened it up and there was a chest full of gems, including the rubies. "You may take some and be on your way."

"Thank you," I cried. I took some rubies and placed it in Zelda's bag.

"You will be carried back just outside the marshlands by two of the guard trolls. It will be a safer journey." We both thanked the leader and two tall muscular trolls came in and picked us up. "Remember, young girl, we are all counting on you to defeat the warlock."

I felt a lead weight hit my body with these words. So much is dependent on my defeating the warlock. We have the rubies, and now I can start building my power, but I have a long way to go. We then headed out of the marshland and onto our magic brooms to head back home.

CHAPTER 7

Despite the lack of sleep, I was much focused. Zelda made the magic potion out of rubies, and I felt energized. I was ready for the training, and I was ready to extinguish the dragon's flame. Mr. Flick gave us all a chalice with a golden burning flame in it.

"I want you all to put out this golden flame with your magic. It looks like a simple task to do, but I assure you it's very difficult," he said. "Now I want you to all take out your magic wands and wave it in a circular motion. I don't want you to chant anything. I want you to imagine the flame getting smaller and smaller until it's gone."

With these instructions, I took out my magic wand and waved it in a small circular motion. I looked at the flame and then imagined it getting smaller and smaller. Nothing happened. I closed my eyes and took a deep breath. I tried it again only in a bigger circular motion. As the flame disappeared, I felt very faint.

"What's the matter with me? I feel very faint," I asked Mr. Flick. "Me too!" everyone else said.

"That's the power of the golden flame. It will drain your energy at first. You will all get used to it hopefully, for you all have to take on the dragon by the end of the week." Mr. Flick waved his magic wand and the chalice lit up again. "Now we'll spend all day doing it again and again."

Zelda gave me more of the ruby potion when I arrived home. I was so tired I barely ate any of the baked vegetables Zelda had made. I went upstairs and soaked in a hot bath and felt so much better. I got changed into my pyjamas and went into my bedroom and started to meditate in which Mr. Flick had assigned us to do to make the next day task easier.

The next day, I felt much better. I had my energy back, and I was ready to do another day's work. Mr. Flick took us all out to the yard where a bush was burning with the golden flame. The bush didn't seem to get eaten up by the flame as a burning bush should. We were told to extinguish the bush using our magic. I took out my wand and waved it around in a large circular motion then imagined the flames getting smaller and smaller. Instantly, the flames started to shrink. I felt a heavy weight on my body as I imagined the flame disappearing. The flames got smaller and smaller. All of a sudden, I felt my legs weaken and I collapsed to the ground. The next thing I remember was waking up on a bed in a small room with a lady in a white uniform injecting me with something with a syringe. "My name is Nurse Rose, and you have been unconscious for most of the day," she said. "What happened?" I asked.

"Well, you passed out after putting out the golden flame. Don't worry, you are human after all, and everyone was surprised you made it this far," said the nurse.

"Oh, I don't know how I'm going to take on the dragon if I pass out." The nurse patted me on the hand in a reassuring way. "Don't worry, the hardest bit is over. It will get easier tomorrow. That's if you're destined to be a powerful witch."

The next day's task was similar. We all had to extinguish a larger bush. I closed my eyes for a few minutes and relaxed. Then I took my magic wand out of my bag, held it firmly, and waved it around. First in a small circular motion and then larger and larger. I focused on the flame going out and then with no trouble at all it went out.

"I did it!" I cried.

"Good work, Bethany. You have now caught up with the rest of the class," said Mr. Flick. I was relieved. I tried it again and with the same results. Mr. Flick then assigned us to a burning tree, and we all put out the flame with no trouble. "It seems you all can handle putting out the flame rather easily today. This is great progress. But I have to warn you, extinguishing the dragon fire will be difficult. He will come at you at full force, and it will drain your energy. The trick is to extinguish the flame as soon as possible," said Mr. Flick. "Okay, if there are no questions, I want you to all go home and spend the rest of the day meditating."

Zelda gave me the rest of the ruby potion after eating scrambled eggs and toast for breakfast. "This last potion will unlock more of your potential," she said.

"Thank you," I replied. I drank the potion and felt more focused than ever. I grabbed my stuff for school and headed off. I arrived twenty minutes earlier than usual for class and found that everyone was earlier than me. I watched Samson and Jade who were killing time by throwing a ball to each other. "It's a focus ball," said Daisy. "You pass it to each other and focusing on the ball helps you to unlock your full potential. It's good, but meditation and a good herbal remedy I had this morning is better."

"Well, everyone seems ready," I replied.

Mr. Flick walked into the room with a bright look on his face. "Well, it's time for your test. I will take you all to the dragon's lair for your challenge, but first I will give you all a potion to drink. It will all protect you from the dragon and his fire from harming you." We all took a small vial of a blue potion and drank. "Now we walk the way. The lair is just past the school grounds in a cave," he said.

It took us an hour of walking to reach the cave. I didn't understand why we didn't use our flying brooms, but I enjoyed the walk. We arrived a few meters from the large dragon's cave. "Now the dragon is tied up inside the cave. I want you to all stay away from the cave while I throw this magic rock inside. The rock will make a high-pitched sound and will get the dragon out of his cave. When the dragon comes out, I want one of you to get close up. When you do, he will breathe the golden fire on you. You will get hit by the flame, but it won't hurt you but will start draining your energy. I want all of you to use your wands and focus on putting out the flame so the dragon can't breathe any more fire. After that, I will restore the dragon so he can breathe fire for the next person to try. Okay then, I want Jade to go first."

Mr. Flick pulled a small black smooth stone out of his pocket, and we all stood far away from cave. After a minute, a big dragon with red scaly skin came out. He just stood there watching us.

"Okay, Jade, now go forth," commanded Mr. Flick. Jade stepped forth and moved closer to the dragon. The dragon let out a roar and breathed fire on Jade, and he fell over. The dragon breathed more fire on Jade, and he lay there not moving.

"We should help him!" I cried. "Get up, Jade! You can't fight the fire while lying down."

Jade started to move then struggled to his feet. His body was weary from the flame but managed to whirl his wand around. The dragon breathed another breath of fire, but it was small this time, not enough to hit Jade. The dragon tried again and this time no fire came out of his mouth.

"He did it!" I cried.

"Okay, Bethany, it's your turn," said Mr. Flick.

I moved forth close to the dragon. Mr. Flick waved his wand and the dragon breathed fire on me. I felt weak but manage to stand strong. The fire was warm and tingly but did not hurt me. I waved my wand in a large circular motion and focused on the flame getting smaller and smaller. The dragon tried to breathe more fire on me but he could not.

"I did it!" I cried.

"Well done, Bethany," said Mr. Flick. After that it was Daisy's turn, then Sampson's, then Ruby's, and they all extinguished the dragon's flame with relative ease.

"Congratulations to you all. You have passed the first test, and you have all proven you are very powerful witches. This will lead you to all privileged places in the league of witches," said Mr. Flick.

Zelda was mixing a cocktail of magic potions as she usually spends her afternoon. "I passed the first test," I said to her.

"I knew you would at least pass fire. Most pass fire, but I better warn you now the rest is much harder."

"I'm so exhausted. I might go have a rest now," I replied. "Go rest up because tomorrow is our quest to get the magic

egg from the red phoenix." I was disappointed. The quest had to be tomorrow because I wanted a day's rest, and I wanted to spend time with Zanda. I went upstairs, changed into my pyjamas, and fell asleep.

CHAPTER 8

"Wake up, Bethany. You have slept in, and we are wasting time," said Zelda, shaking me awake. I got up and had a quick shower and changed into appropriate clothes for another adventure. I went downstairs and had toast with jam for breakfast.

"We are going to the outskirts of the Black Forest. We are heading to the giant trees of the forest where the red phoenix has her nest. We are going to ask for one of her eggs. If we are lucky, she will give us one but not without a favour. That's if we are lucky."

"It sounds a lot better than wandering the marshlands," I replied. I finished my breakfast, grabbed our flying broom, and then took off. It was over three hour's flight until I saw the giant trees. The trees were narrow and tall as we were flying.

"We stop here and walk on foot," said Zelda. We landed and walked for hours in the forest without seeing anything.

"This seems like a peaceful part of the forest," I said. "There are no dangerous animals here."

"That's a relief," I replied.

"Okay, we stop here. Her nest is around here, and she is probably hunting. We wait for now and have some lunch." Zelda unpacked a couple of egg sandwiches to eat. I ate my food then buried myself amongst the grass and fell asleep.

"Wake up!" cried Zelda. I woke up not knowing how long I've been asleep. "I see the phoenix in the distance. I have a whistle that will call for the phoenix to come." I looked and saw a red dot in the sky, assuming that it was the red phoenix. Zelda blew the whistle, but I did not hear anything. The dot came closer and closer until I could make out it was a bird. She flew closer and closer until she landed in front of us. She was a beautiful bird with feathers of crimson red and about half our length.

"What do you want?" she said.

"We want one of your eggs to make a magic potion." "Go away. I don't give away my eggs to witches."

"Please, great phoenix. I am human, training to be a witch. I need your egg to enhance my powers to defeat the evil warlock."

"I don't like that warlock. He and the king have been cutting down some of the trees with nests in them."

"When I defeat him, I will pledge to the king to stop the destruction of the trees. Right now, the warlock controls the king."

"Very well, if it's for a good cause, but you have to do me a favour first."

"Yes! Anything!"

"It just so happens the giant from the north has taken some of my eggs. If you can bring them back and stop him from taking it again, I will let you have one of my eggs."

"We can do that for you," Zelda interrupted. "He's about an hour's walk from here." We thanked the red phoenix and headed off. We walked for an hour north and saw the giant sitting down and resting with a basket of the phoenix eggs. I went up to him and tapped him on the leg. He looked at me with surprise.

"What do you want, little ones?"

"I'm on a quest to retrieve the eggs that you have taken from the red phoenix and give them back to her."

"Go away. They're mine. I will squash you like a bug if you try to take the eggs." He stood up and they realized he was as tall as the trees.

"I am training to be a very powerful witch. If you don't give them back and stop taking the eggs, I will cast a spell on you."

He laughed. "I am not afraid of witches." He started to walk way, and I casted a paralyses spell so he couldn't walk.

"Set me free!" cried the giant.

I sent a shock spell to his hand, and he dropped the basket. Zelda ran up to the eggs and touched all but one egg, and they disappeared. "I teleported the eggs back to the phoenix. One is for us." Zelda took the egg and gave it to me. It was big, and the shell was a light pink. "Watch out!" cried Zelda.

The giant was free from the spell and had his leg up to step on me. I quickly responded by creating a force field around Zelda and I to prevent the giant from crushing us. The weight of the giant's foot was putting a lot of pressure on the field and draining my energy.

"I don't know how long I can hold this!" I cried.

"I'll hold the field while you eat the egg. You will need your full potential to shrink the giant."

"Okay," I replied. I cracked the egg carefully in half and held the yolk in one side of the shell. I ate the yolk and it tasted terrible. I felt more energized and focused on the giant getting smaller and smaller.

Almost instantly, the giant started to shrink. Smaller and smaller he went until he was only a bit taller than the tallest man, which it very small compared to what he was.

"What have you done to me!" cried the giant.

"I had to cast a powerful spell on you. You would have crushed us," I replied. The giant covered his hands over his face and started to cry. "Oh, don't cry," I said, "it's only a temporary spell. You will grow and become a giant again. However, if you keep taking the eggs, you will shrink again, and it will be permanent."

"Oh thank goodness," replied the giant. "I won't take the eggs again," he said and then walked off.

"Come on, Bethany, you have consumed the magic egg and now it time to head home."

CHAPTER 9

I woke up from a deep sleep by a tap on the bedroom door. "Yes," I mumbled sleepily. Zelda walked in. "It's ten o'clock.
You slept in. Anyway, it doesn't matter. Zanda is here waiting for you."

"Oh, I desperately want to see him," I replied. I got myself up and found my body weak, and I felt hungry. I hopped in the shower and changed into a skirt and blouse I've been saving for a nice occasion. I walked downstairs and saw Zanda sitting at the breakfast table drinking an orange juice.

"Hello, Beth," he said.

"Hi. What are you doing here?" I replied.

"Well, it's my day off, and I was hoping to take you on a picnic."

"That's a great idea. I could do with a relaxing day with all the hard work that I've been doing."

"I made you some toast with jam. I want you to eat before you go," said Zelda. I sat down and ate the toast then drank a cup of orange juice.

"You must be proud of Beth for passing her first test," Zanda said to Zelda.

"That was the easiest. She's yet to pass the rest," she replied. "Well, I finished my toast and juice. Let's go," I interrupted.

We both left and entered the cart.

"We are going to the countryside just past the stables," said Zanda. We took off with only the horse guiding us. I told Zanda about all my adventures on the way. He congratulated me on passing the test and reminded me that I was already a powerful witch and that I could take the binding bracelet off and go home.

"It's not time yet," I said. "I need to try and defeat the warlock. People are dependent on me now." I talked more on how I got the magic egg and more on what's expected of me now. I talked for so long that I missed the scenery of the countryside, and we arrived at our destination in what seemed like no time at all.

"We've arrived. Let's enjoy the walk in the countryside and we can talk more later." Zanda said. He picked up the picnic basket and we left the cart. We walked in silence with us holding hands. I noticed an amazing bird life in the countryside with rolling hills with grass so green. We walked for an hour before we stopped.

"Let's stop for an early lunch," said Zanda. "Good idea. I'm hungry," I replied.

He laid out a big blanket on the ground. Then he unpacked a flask of tea and sandwiches. I unwrapped the foil of the sandwich and noticed it had ham. "Oh, Zanda! Ham!" I cried. "Yes, that's right. It was hard to get, but I thought you would like some meat for a change." "Yes. Thank you, Zanda."

We ate the sandwich and drank the tea, and it was so good. After that we sat in silence enjoying the scenery. After a while, I felt a little tired and lay down on the blanket. Zanda gave a big yawn and lay down close next to me, wrapping his arms around me.

"So tell me more about your adventures."

"I've said enough. You tell me something now." "What do you want to know?"

"Tell me your desires?" I said. "You're my desire," he said.

"No. I mean a dream you have. What do you want to do besides tending to the horses?"

"Well," he said, "the king holds a horse race on at the palace. Both witches and humans can enter the race, and there is a big festival included. It's held once every five years, and the next one is at the end of this year."

"Are you going to enter?" I questioned. "I hope so. It's hard to get in, but I'll try."

"Maybe when I become the most powerful witch, I can ask the king to favour you."

"Oh, thank you, Bethany," he replied and gave me a big hug. We packed up our leftovers and continued on with the walk with me as happy as ever.

CHAPTER 10

"Now listen up," said Mr. Flick. "This week, we are learning how to control water. Water is a complicated element for a witch to master and requires a lot of energy. We will be controlling the weather and mastering the art of forming rain clouds. You might be thinking that controlling the weather is reasonably easy for a witch to achieve. But when you're tested, you will be bringing forth rain clouds and making it rain bubbles. Because it is unnatural, it is hard for a witch to master. Now today, we are going to the pond outside to form bubbles."

"That sound like fun," said Jade.

We all left the class and went to the pond at the back of the school.

"Now we are going to achieve something exciting today. We are going to form a bubble around ourselves and then we will fly off," said Mr. Flick. Everyone laughed with excitement.

I got out my magic wand and stood in the pond. I waved my wand around and focused on a bubble forming around me. Instantly, the water formed a bubble around me, and I started to fly away. I rose high up, and the wind started to move me far away from the school. I focused on controlling the bubble, so I wouldn't fly far. I moved around, heading back to the pond then descended and landed on the ground till the bubble popped.

"Well, it seems like everyone had no trouble with the task. I expect that you will all master water by the end of it," said Mr. Flick. "Now I want you to all get to know each other over the lunch break."

Sampson was the last one to land and then we all headed off to the cafeteria together. It was still half an hour before the lunch bell, but it would give me enough time to get to know everyone before Zanda arrived.

I chose pumpkin soup at the cafeteria, and everyone else had slug pie. I couldn't think of anything more gross. I sat down in between Ruby and Daisy with Sampson and Jade on the other side of the table.

"Well, I think we are all going to master water," said Sampson to everyone.

"I hope we all can pass all of them," said Ruby.

"Well, there can be only one castor three. I hope that will be me," said Jade.

"Well, I think Beth has done well for a human," said Sampson.

"A bit too well," said Jade.

"A human too can be a powerful witch, and Beth is clever," replied Daisy, defending me.

"As long as we are all good, it doesn't matter who will be the next caster three witch," said Ruby.

"Well said, Ruby. We all have to use our power for good otherwise we will be banished. Unfortunately, warlocks can get away with more than witches," said Daisy.

"Why is that?" I asked.

"Well, witches have a council of witches to monitor their behaviour. Warlocks don't have such a council," said Daisy.

"Why?" I asked.

"It is thought that witches' magic come from the underworld. Dark witches come from dark spirits and can bring on these spirits into this world. To prevent this, the council of witches have been set up to prevent witches from using their power for dark purposes. Warlocks are different. Their power comes from nature and more naturally. Unless the warlock is behaving too badly, nothing happens to them."

"Well, I think this warlock is behaving badly," I replied. "Yeah, I think we are just putting up with more and more," said Sampson.

After talking for a while, the bell rang to go back to class, and I had forgotten about Zanda. We had self-defence, and we had a day of skirmish. After that, I was tired and was relieved when I got back to Zelda's. I ate my dinner that she prepared for me and told her about my day.

I went to bed an hour early that normal, and I had a dream that I was lost in the Black Forest. I met a man in his forties with long black hair and long black beard. He had grey-coloured eyes and sagging eyelids. I asked him his name and replied that he had no name, but everyone referred to him as the warlock. He told me that it was no good challenging him and that I should go home.

I woke up the next day feeling the weight of the world on my shoulders. I told Zelda about my dream and explained that working with water can be tiring to a witch and gave me a natural remedy to help me.

The rest of the day was filled with us forming rain clouds over the school. The next day was us forming snow cloud and letting it snow over the school. That was a particularly fun day for the school took a break to play in the snow. I woke up on Thursday with a sore throat and my head spinning. Zelda thought it was best to spend the day in bed. I spent all day drifting in and out of sleep. When I slept, I had dreams of being lost in the forest and all forest creatures were after me. On Friday was the day of the test.

We all gathered at the school grounds and each took turns making it rain bubbles. It wasn't easy, but we all passed the test and celebrated with cake at the cafeteria after.

"Well done," said Mr. Flick. "Next, we will be learning to master earth. And if you can all pass the test, you will all be placed on the council of witches."

CHAPTER 11

It was early Saturday morning when Zanda came and visited. "I thought we would celebrate by me taking you out on a boat ride at Witches' Lake," he said. "I didn't know there was a Witches' Lake." "Oh yes. It's some distance away, but witches often go and visit there."

"Oh, I'm not sure if I can handle a long ride on the broom." "That's okay. We'll take Snow. He will get us there in no time," he replied. "Fabulous!"

It took an hour for Snow to reach the lake. He took us to a wharf where there were two rowing boats tied up. We hopped on one of the rowing boats, untied the rope, and took off with Zanda rowing while I sat and relaxed.

"You know I can just use my magic to row the boat," I said. "No, that's fine. I need the exercise." As he rowed the boat,

I noticed it was a sunny day with light winds, which helped the boat along. He took us out to the middle of the lake, and as he stopped rowing, the winds died down.

"It's like everything around us knows we are here," I said. "It does. The winds and the mountains here are alive," he replied.

"Oh, Zanda, there's so much I don't understand. I don't know if I'm suitable to be on the council of witches."

"They will teach you all you need to know," he replied, "and besides it's just a meeting three times a year. You can live at home and be on the council."

I felt reassured by his words and smiled. I was about to say to Zanda that it was going to be alright, but I was distracted by a loud screech. I looked over to the left and saw a large black- and-white bird heading for us.

"It's one of the king's pet birds called a messenger bird," Zanda explained.

"That's a funny name for a bird," I replied. The bird perched himself on the boat, and we watched him for a minute or so, then he spoke.

"I have a message for Bethany," said the bird in a human male voice.

"How peculiar," I replied.

"It's the voice of the warlock. He has sent the bird to give you a message."

"Go home," continued the bird. "You don't belong with the witches, and you cannot defeat me. So if you know what is good for you, young girl, you will stop using your powers and go home where you belong."

"Go away, bird!" shouted Zanda. The bird then flew off. "What was that all about?" I said.

"I don't know, but the warlock does not like you using your powers."

I wondered why he gave me that message and then wondered if he could be right.
"Let's go home," I said.
"Okay," he replied, and he rowed us back to the wharf.

CHAPTER 12

"Earth is the most important element to master, even more important than air. There is a special type of rock called iron rock. You will all have to learn how to carve an image of yourselves out of this rock, and if you are meant to be on the council of witches, your image will stay."

"What do you mean?" questioned Jade.

"You will have two days to carve an image of yourself on these special rocks, and if the image is still there the next day, you have passed. If not, the rock will crumble into sand and you have failed.

"Why isn't this the last part of the test if earth is more important than air?" asked Daisy.

"Good question, Daisy. To be on the council, your powers must have Theta rays in them and can only be determined in this special rock." Mr. Flick opened the classroom cupboard door and pulled out a big trolley with five large red stone two meters each in dimension. Then he pulled out five large mirrors and place each one in front of us.

"Now, I don't expect each of you to be an artist but with the mirror and your magic, you will carve an image of yourselves into the rock. This takes time, so I have given you by the end of tomorrow to finish it. The next day, you will come to class to see which rock survives. After that, the ones who have passed the test will listen to a guest speaker."

"Guest speaker?" I questioned.

"Yes," said Mr. Flick. "The head of the witches' council, Gwen, will give a lecture on what is excepted of you as a member of the council." He paused and smiled at us before placing the rock in front of us then gave the command to begin sculpting.

It was a slow process. We all started with the chin and worked our way up, and by the end of the day, we had completed half of our lower faces, finishing off with the nose.

That night I had a peaceful sleep. The most peaceful I had in a long time. I woke up feeling happy and focused and ready to finish my sculpture. Sculpting had been easier today than yesterday, but it was still a slow process. We all had finished between three and four o'clock in the afternoon that day, and we were relieved.

I had arrived at Zelda's an hour early than normal and discovered Zelda had finished making a cake.

"It's a celebration cake," she said. "I heard humans eat cake to celebrate occasions."

"Why, yes. Thank you. Although I won't know the results of my test until tomorrow," I said.

"It doesn't matter. To make it this far is incredible, and now, whatever will be will be." I smiled and Zelda handed me the knife, and I cut the cake, making a wish for the sculpture to be intact the next day.

As soon as we all arrived at class, Mr. Flick went into the store room to get the sculpture. He pulled out the trolley, and we saw that there were four objects covered with canvas. We all gasped knowing that one of us failed the test. Mr. Flick uncovered one canvas, and we all saw Daisy's sculpture fully intact. Daisy let out a shriek, and we all clapped. He uncovered another, and we saw Sampson's rock intact and clapped. He uncovered another one and saw that Jade's sculpture was intact. We clapped. I was feeling pretty low, positive that I was the one who failed. Mr. Flick uncovered the last one, and we were all amazed to see that my sculpture survived.

"Sorry, Ruby," said Mr. Flick. "Your rock turned to sand. This means you have failed." We all fell silent and gave Ruby a hug.

"This is ridiculous!" shouted Jade. "It should have been Bethany."

"Sorry?" said Mr. Flick.

"Bethany should have not gotten this far, and it's not natural to have a human to be on the council of witches. She must have cheated!"

"You cannot cheat in this test," explained Mr. Flick. "You either have Theta rays or not." I felt as though Jade was right. How could I have such power? Is this natural?"

There was a knock on the door. Mr. Flick opened the door. It was an elderly woman wearing a traditional witch's cloak and hat.

"Hi, Gwen," said Mr. Flick. "All but one has passed earth.

A fine student named Ruby has failed the test."

"Don't be disappointed," Gwen said to Ruby, "you still have the privilege to do research for the council. That's if you want to."

Ruby smiled. "Oh yes, I think research would be the most interesting job I could do." Gwen smiled and shook Ruby's hand. "Then that is settled. Go to your previous class, and I will talk more about it then." Ruby smiled and thanked all of us for being supportive then left.

Over the next few hours, Gwen gave us a lecture on our responsibilities as a council member. After that, Mr. Flick spoke to us about the last test air!

"Air is the final part of the elements we will test. For this part, you will use air to fly without any broom. This is an easy task to learn, but what will be difficult is that once you have learned the task, you will use air to race each other. You will race each other three laps around the school. The witch that comes last will fail."

Mr. Flick gave a moments paused then continued, "Gwen will give you each a book to study, and you can practice at home. We will commence back on Monday morning, and you will be tested. Congratulations to all who passed. I will see you on Monday."

It was lunchtime when I arrived back at Zelda's, and she made me a vegetarian lasagne. I ate it all up then told her the good news.

"It is time to complete your next quest. You will need to convince the oyster to give you his magic pearl. For this quest, he will ask you to do something for him. The lake in which he lives in is polluted with the warlock's waste that comes from mixing his potions. He will ask you to clean it up."

"That doesn't sound hard," I said.

"Oh, but this will be the hardest spell you've ever done. To remove his waste from the lake requires special qualities."

"What do you mean? "I asked.

"It's not enough to be a powerful witch. You must possess certain qualities to do this spell, and it is rare in witches."

"What qualities? "I said.

"You must possess a high level of bravery and selflessness for this spell to work."

"And this is rare in witches?"

"Witches can be brave, but we are quiet selfish in nature."

I didn't think so. "Why do you need these qualities to clean up a river?"
"Because the waste comes from a warlock's power that is cowardly and selfish."
"I see," I said.
"We can't waste any more time. We will go tomorrow to Lake Ayre."

CHAPTER 13

It was early in the morning when we arrived at the lake. The water was grey and murky. "You must use your powers to clean up the lake," said Zelda. "There is a large oyster at the bottom of the lake. Once the lake is clean, you must ask the oyster for his pearl. There's no guarantee he will give it to you."

"I will do my best," I replied.

"Now think of a time that you were selfless and brave and cast your magic on to the water."

I closed my eyes and thought about any time that I felt brave and selfless. I thought about my life at Sandsdale and then my life as a witch but couldn't think of a time where I did a brave and selfless act.

"It's no use. I don't think I am brave and selfless," I said to Zelda.

"My girl, I think you are the bravest and most selfless person and witch I know. Think of the time you saved Sandsdale from draught in exchange for becoming an apprentice," she said.

"I guess you're right," I replied. "I know I'm right! Now focus!"

I picked up my wand and waved it around in circles, closed my eyes, and thought of the time I met Zelda and agreed to live a life as a witch. I felt a euphoric sensation run through my body.

"It worked," said Zelda.

I opened my eyes and saw that the lake was clear with a pale blue tinge to it. I smiled. "Now use your aquatic spell to walk to the bottom of the lake and talk to the oyster," said Zelda.

I cast the spell and walked into the water. I felt like I was made out of lead and that I was breathing oxygen from under water. The water was deep, but I was walking on the bottom with no problems. I saw the biggest oyster about half my size.

"Hello," I spoke clearly. "Hello," the oyster replied.

"I have come to ask you if I can have your pearl," I asked "I need it to help defeat the warlock that has been polluting the lake."

"There's no point of having my pearl because you are not powerful enough to defeat the warlock."

I looked at the oyster in a peculiar way. "How do you know this?"

"Don't get me wrong, you probably will master the elements, but there is something getting in your way," he said

"What?" I asked.

"I sense you have a lot of fear in you. Am I right?"

"Well there's a lot of pressure defeating the warlock, and I've been having bad dreams."

"Well, this fear will prevent you from using your full potential, and you won't be powerful enough to stop the warlock."

CHAPTER 14

I woke up especially early Monday morning. Zelda was already in the kitchen preparing the last of the pearl tonic. "Here you go, Bethany. Drink up." I drank the tonic and felt relaxed and focused. After that, Zelda made me pancakes, and we engaged in idle chit-chat, talking about all the things I can do now that I'm part of the council of witches.

The early morning passed by quickly, and I arrived on time for the big race. It was nine o'clock, and we all went out on to the oval. We cast our spell that used the wind to pick us up. The force of wind is what will take us around the circuit at full speed.

"I want you to do three laps around the school and remember to stay in between the flags," said Mr. Flick. We all hovered in a line preparing ourselves to take off. "Ready," he paused. "Set." He waited until we looked focused. "Go!"

We all took off at rapid speed. A half a kilometre in and Daisy was in front, way ahead while Jade, Sampson and I were clustered together. I bypassed Jade then Sampson bypassed me, and we took in turns bypassing each other, while Daisy was way ahead of us after the first lap. After the second lap, I was way ahead of Jade and Sampson and was catching up to Daisy. We were on our third lap, and I was very close to Daisy but I didn't have the power she had. Jade and Sampson were far behind. Jade was last and Sampson was second last. We almost completed our third lap, and Daisy was still ahead and was first to cross the line. I came second. Jade and Sampson were neck to neck until Jade moved forward and came third and then Sampson fourth.

We moved in front of Mr. Flick and landed with ease. "Well done!" cried Mr. Flick. "Sorry, Sampson, you didn't master air so you cannot move on to the next stage. However, you will now be placed on the witches' council."

"It's what I always wanted," he replied.

"Gwen will meet you in the hall now." He thanked everyone and headed off.

"Okay, everyone, it's time to get started on the next part of your testing."

"What's that?" questioned Jade.

"You will learn all the skills and spells that you can master to defeat the warlock."

"How long will this take?" I asked.

"You will challenge the warlock in three weeks' time."

I gave a big sigh hoping it would be enough time to work on my other quest as well.

I went to bed straight after dinner and fell asleep straight away. I found myself walking in the Black Forest. Everything sounded peaceful, and I was picking berries for my mother. It had been a long day, and I started to head back home. I saw the omen bird as I did before, and I went to say hello.

"Hello, omen bird," I said.

It spoke back in a deep voice, "You cannot defeat me." I walked away in a hurry. As I walked, I saw a deer. "You cannot defeat me," it said. I walked away from the deer and walked faster and faster deep in the forest. My heart started to pound then I felt the Black Forest come alive. "You cannot defeat me," said the voices coming from all around. I placed my hands over my ears and I started to run.

As I ran, the voices became louder and louder. I fell over a tree root sticking up from the ground. I fell on my face and slowly picked myself up. There was the warlock in front of me pointing his wand at me.

"I am more powerful than you," he said. "If you don't go home, I will kill you!" he screamed. He waved the wand and a force so powerful knocked me off my feet. The next thing I knew I was in bed, and it was day.

I managed to climb out of bed feeling sore all over as though I really fell in the forest. I headed to the kitchen and saw Zelda making breakfast.

"How is the most powerful witch in the village today?" said Zelda in a good mood.

"I don't feel like a powerful witch today, Zelda," I replied, looking glum.

"What's the matter?"

"I had another nightmare, and if I don't let go of my fears, I won't be able to beat the warlock."

"You're paying too much attention to that oyster. Fear is a normal witch and human emotion."

"I know, but the warlock is really getting to me. He threatened to kill me in my dreams."

Zelda rubbed me on the back, and I felt better. "Look, Bethany. I think you should talk to Gwen for advice."

"Okay," I replied. "I only have a half a day of defence practice today. I will pay a visit to the council after."

CHAPTER 15

After a morning of learning how to deflect attacks from freeze rays and energy photons, I met up with Zanda at the cafeteria.

"How's the super witch today?" he said.

"Well I learnt today I have to work on my reflexes, and I've got to talk to Gwen after lunch to learn how to control my fears."

"Fears?" he questioned.

"Yes, I am afraid of the warlock, and I have so many other fears, Zanda."

"We all have fears, Beth, it's natural. Maybe all you have to do is try not let it take hold of you."

"Yes, you're probably right."

Zanda took my hand and wrapped it in his big hands. "You're the most fearless person I know. I don't think you have much of a problem."

I gave him a big hug, and I felt better. "I better go now and talk to Gwen," I said. I gave Zanda another big hug and left the cafeteria and headed to the conference room where Gwen was giving a speech to council members.

I sat in on the last half an hour of the speech. Gwen was explaining how we must identify evil in all aspects of life. She explained evil spirits can walk with witches, humans, trolls, warlocks, and much more who do evil acts. She added that it's up to the witches to send the evil spirits back to the underworld in which they came from. After the speech drew to a conclusion, we took a break for some afternoon tea and conversation. I headed to get some coffee where Gwen was heading.

"Bethany! What a nice surprise to see you here," said Gwen. "That was an interesting speech you made."

"Why, thank you. This was only optional but have almost all witches on the council today."

"Yes, that's great." I paused to gather my next thoughts. "Gwen, there's something I need to talk to you about."

"Yes, what is it?" she said.

"I've been having nightmares about the warlock and wolves and being lost in the Black Forest."

"It's okay. They are only dreams," Gwen reassured me.

"I was told that my fears are affecting my full potential enough so that the warlock will defeat me."

"Fear can weaken you, but only if the fear is overwhelming you," she said.

"I think it is," I added.

"There are ways you can control the fear." "How?" I said.

"Talk to a dream guidance counsellor." "Where do I find one?"

"Why, it so happens the best dream counsellor is Jade's uncle." Gwen's eyes darted around the room. "There he is talking to Sampson next to the water fountain. Go talk to him, Beth."

I sighed in disappointment. "What's wrong?" queried Gwen.

"Jade doesn't like me very much. He doesn't believe a human should be on the council."

"Oh that's silly. We will go over and talk to him together." That didn't ease my confidence, but I agreed. We walked over to Jade and Sampson.

"Hello, gentlemen," said Gwen to both Jade and Sampson. "Hello, Gwen," they both replied at once.

"Jade, can Beth and I speak to you alone?" "Um?" replied Jade.

"It's okay, Jade, I have to go to class now anyway," said Sampson.

"Yes, what is it?" questioned Jade, trying not to sound rude. "Beth needs a dream guidance counsellor, and I thought you could ask your Uncle Ron to give Beth some counselling.

"Well, he is er... He is very busy," replied Jade.

"It's important," demanded Gwen. "Beth has been having nightmares about the warlock and it's affecting her power."

"I don't think my uncle can help her," he stated. "I think he can."

"It's no use. Leave him alone," I interrupted.

"No, Beth. It's important that Jade's uncle try and help you." Gwen sighed and gave Jade a pat on the shoulder. "Don't you want to help Beth?" she asked Jade.

He bowed his head and then raised it, giving out a serious look on his face. "No I don't!" he said firmly.

"Why?" Gwen demanded.

"Because Beth was not meant to come this far, let alone be the most powerful witch there is."

"But why not?" asked Gwen. "You know as well as I that humans can make just as powerful witches as a natural-born witch."

Jade thought for a moment then he revealed, "A few years ago my uncle and I went to see the prophet snake in the mountains. She predicted that I could become the most powerful witch of them all if it wasn't for an unnatural force standing in my way."

"And you think Beth is that unnatural force?" said Gwen. "Yes," replied Jade.

"Well, I think your selfishness is the thing standing in your way."

"Selfishness?"

"Usually, it is our own faults that prevent us being all powerful. Sure, you can have blue magic and pass the test of element, but is it a personal fault of a witch that has prevented a witch obtaining his or her full powerful? Don't worry about who's going to beat the warlock. Improve on yourself and you will do the best you can."

Jade bowed his head for a moment in thought then raised his head, showing a tear in his eye. "Okay," he said, "my uncle can help you. In fact, he's not doing much this Saturday and spending time with me. Can you come to Twelve Avenue Hill on Saturday at ten?" Jade asked me.

"Yes! I can," I replied with joy. "Great! See you then."

CHAPTER 16

I arrived at a small cottage on Avenue Hill exactly at ten. I knocked on the door, and it opened straight away. Jade greeted me on the other side of the door. It was morning teatime, and he offered me some dried fruit and peppermint tea.

"Uncle Ron said these refreshments will help you to relax." "Where is your uncle now?" I asked.

"He's at the market buying some candles for our meditation session. He will be back any minute now."

I sat there in silence for ten minutes sipping my peppermint tea while Jade pulled out a record player and played some ancient witches' folk music.

"It's beautiful," I said to Jade, listening to the music.

"The music will help you tap into your subconscious. It is the root of your fears." I heard the front door open followed by a hello from an elderly man. "Hi, Uncle Ron!" shouted Jade. "Bethany is here!"

A man with long grey hair and very wrinkled face came into the kitchen.

"Hi, I'm Bethany Hardings," I said, introducing myself to him. "Call me Ron," he replied.

"Nice to meet you, Ron."

Ron held a bag in his hand and pulled out two beeswax candles from it. "Just give me five minutes to set up and then we'll begin."

He walked off and came back ten minutes later. "It's time to do our meditation. Please go to the end of the corridor into the meditation room."

I walked into the room. The room was dimly lit, and the candles that were burning provided most of the light.

"Take a seat on the cushion," Ron said. I sat down on a big green cushion on the floor. "Just relax, Bethany," he said. I took a deep breath in and out slowly and felt my body relax. "I had Gwen pay me a visit yesterday and told me about your fears. I feel that your fears are retracting your powers. I could sense that when I walked in the door."

"Can you help me?" I said.

"Yes I can," he replied with full confidence. "We need to do a long meditation session. I will talk to you while you close your eyes and concentrate. Let my voice guide you."

"Okay," I replied.

"Sit comfortably and close your eyes and we shall begin." I crossed my legs, resting my hands on my lap and closed my eyes.

"I want you to clear your mind and focus on what I'm saying," continued Ron. "Just let your mind be in suspension for a few minutes." I cleared my mind and found myself floating. "Imagine that you are flying high in the air amongst the clouds. You are flying in a very safe place now." I felt myself flying in the air and felt safe. "Now you see your home village and you land down to meet your friends." I imagined me landing in front of my home where Tom and Mum were. "You feel safe and happy, and now you bid them farewell because your journey is not over. You take off again and you are flying safely in the air once more." I felt a bit sad for leaving mum and Tom but felt very safe in the air. "Now below, you see the Black Forest and you hear it greet you." I felt a bit tense but still okay. "You see a small patch in where you land safely. You are in the Black Forest and you feel no danger. All around you are trees and you hear birds chirping. You look up and you see the night sky. The moon lights your path and you start walking. As you walk, you see birds and racoons in the trees. You hear something howl in the distance, but you are not afraid. You keep walking and your surroundings get brighter. You look up to the sky and see a bright star. You focus on the star and you feel strong. You look into the star and notice it's beaming a white light onto you. The energy it's giving is giving you special powers. You realise that nothing in the forest can hurt you. In fact, you are friends of all things in the forest. You look down and notice a force field of white around you. You start to walk in the forest and notice all the animals bowing to you. Wolves come out of the forest to meet you. You are not afraid of them. They are your friends. The wolves come up to you and lick your hand and you start to laugh. The wolves see something behind you, and they run away. You turn around and you see the warlock. He does not scare you. He says to you, 'Do not challenge me.' You are not scared of him, and you tell him to leave and never come back. With this request, he disappears and you are now in a field with no one around. You call out my name and then say you are free from fear. You see me and you take my hand and we fly off together. All of a sudden, there is blackness. Nothing around you but space. You feel in control and ready to come home. Now, Bethany, empty your mind and listen to the music as I play the record."

The music started to play. It was the same one I listened to earlier.

"Okay, Bethany, open your eyes." I opened my eyes and saw Ron and the meditation room and felt relaxed. "We are done, Bethany," said Ron.

"That was amazing. Am I free from nightmares?"

"Yes, but you need more work. You need to meditate every evening and make sure you focus on the bright star."

"What is the star?"

"The star is the source of all witches' power. It gives you power, and if you are ever in danger, close your eyes and focus on it. It will keep you safe."

CHAPTER 17

It was another day of defence class, and we spent the morning shooting stun rays at a moving flying ball. It was very difficult. The ball was very small and was always moving, but we were supposed to learn about precision. I was exhausted after the morning's class, and I couldn't wait to have lunch with Zanda. I ordered a salad sandwich and a cup of hot chocolate and sat next to him. "Hello, Zanda," I said.

"Hi, Beth, how was your morning?" he replied.

"Tired and grumpy. We shot stun rays at moving balls in which it has drained all my energy."

"Well, I've got something that may cheer you up." "Oh?" I replied.

"In witches' customs, we tend to get married at twenty- one." "Well, you're only seventeen." I laughed.

"Yes, but we can get engaged at any age."

"Oh yeah?" I replied in wonder. He stretched out his arms and opened his hands. In his hands was a plain silver ring. "It's lovely!" I shrieked.

"I know it's a long wait, but will you be my fiancee?" "Oh, yes!" I cried.

"Fantastic," he replied. "We can wait as long as we want to get married, but I want to marry you when we are both ready." "Oh, I can't wait till I tell everyone," I said. "Mum's going to freak out."

"She will be pleased with you and so proud." We spent the rest of the lunchtime talking about our wedding plans and decided to go for a traditional witches' ceremony rather than a human one. Mum would be disappointed, but it was important to Zanda.

The end of the day couldn't come sooner. I burst in the door and shouted, "Guess what?" to Zelda who was cooking pumpkin soup.

"Yes, my dear?" she replied. "Zanda asked me to marry him."

"That's fantastic!" she shrieked. She turned around and her face appeared very grey.

"What's wrong?" I asked.

"I've got something to tell you. Please sit down, my dear." I sat down with a worried feeling running deep. "I think you and Zanda should go back to Sandsdale."

"Now?" I queried.

"The sooner, the better."

"But I'm ready to challenge the warlock," I replied. "What's this about?" I asked.

"Well, Bethany, the warlock came to me in a dream." "When?" I asked.

"I was taking a nap an hour ago and the warlock appeared."

"It was just a nightmare," I reassured her.

"No, it was the warlock. I can tell. He threatened to kill you if you challenge him."

"He won't kill me, and I am not scared of him anymore." "It's not just that."

"What else?" I replied.

"It's my fault that I put too much pressure on you." "Nonsense," I replied.

"I wanted you to work for me and that was selfish of me. I should have left you alone to tend to your mother."

"Listen to me. Getting to know you and all the other witches was the best thing that's ever happened to me. Being even this powerful, let alone the possibility of most powerful, is amazing because I can make a difference to witches and to humans."

"I just want you to be safe." "I will."

"Okay then, you have my blessing."

"Thank you," I replied and then gave her a hug. "I'm heading to bed. It's been a long day."

"Okay. I will bring up soup. It's important not to skip a meal while you are training."

After an hour of meditation, I ate my soup then went straight to bed. I dreamt I was lost in the Black Forest and was walking, afraid of my situation. Birds sung and I saw deer playing and then felt less afraid. Suddenly a wolf came out and looked at me with curiosity.

"Hello, my friend," I said to it.

The wolf turned in to a huntsman. "Are you lost?" he said.

"Yes, I am," I replied.

"Don't worry, I know the way." I walked with him, and he guided me to the river where I drank the water.

"Can you take me back to Sandsdale?" I said. "Yes," he replied and then I felt calm and safe.

I woke up the next day thinking about the huntsman. I explain the dream to Zelda, and she told me that animals transforming to humans are spirit guides. She told me that whenever you feel lost, spirit guides show you the way. She also told me that they appear to only those who have been on spiritual pilgrimages and said that a very spiritual meditation can be classed as one. "If you are meeting your spirit guide, you are then ready for the challenge of your life."

CHAPTER 18

Today was the day of the contest. The rules of the contest are that each of us wander through the Black Forest and follow a pathway that would lead to the warlock's hideaway. While we are wandering, holograms of the warlock would appear and use his power to stun us then trap us in a yellow force field. Once we are trapped, the game is over. The game is won if we find the true warlock and trap him in a blue force field. The game is not easy. Even if we do find him, he would use his very powerful magic to prevent him being trapped in the force field.

We all congregated just outside of the Black Forest. Eyes were on Jade as he was the first to enter the quest. He was followed by a hovering camera so the spectators could watch him. He walked for half an hour through the Black Forest with no signs of trouble. He had to look very closely on the markers on the ground to find his way. This could distract him if he got fired upon. It's important to have full concentration. All of a sudden, a wolf appeared out of nowhere. Jade froze as the wolf came closer. He managed to fire a stun ray and knocked the wolf out before the wolf could pounce. Then a hologram warlock appeared from behind and knocked him out with a stun ray from his wand. He then trapped Jade in a yellow force field and the match was over. The first attack from a hologram and the match was over. This made me feel defeated.

Next up was Daisy. I believed if anyone could win this, it would be Daisy. Her reflexes were fast, and her power was stronger than mine. She was sent to the Black Forest were she walked along the path with caution. It wasn't long until the first hologram appeared firing a stun ray. With Daisy's quick reflexes, she blocked the ray and fired a special ray to destroy the hologram.

She wandered for hours, and during that time, many holograms made cunning moves to attack her, but she defended all of them. My heart was pounding.

She can win this, I thought.

After a while, it became quiet. No holograms were firing on her and no wolf was trying to pounce. She was close to the real warlock. She came across a large wooden hut. She entered the hut, and the warlock was there waiting for her. Daisy fired a stun ray, but the warlock blocked it with ease. She used other tactics like blind spells and trance curse, but the warlock counteracted all her moves. The warlock fired some kind of force ray, which knocked her off her feet and then fired a freeze ray, which rendered her helplessly immobile. He then successfully trapped her in the yellow force field, and the game for her was lost.

I shuddered in fear for I was next. I was taken to the depths of the Black Forest. I saw the beginning of my path and found it was heading in the opposite direction to where Daisy headed. I heard wolves howl in the distance, and I could feel all the animals in the forest watching me. I was walking and watching closely. Nothing came at me, and the forest grew darker and the trees thicker. I made the end of my wand glow to see my way around. The dark backdrop was another tactic of the warlock. It made it harder for me to see my target and my way around. *Just stay focused, Bethany*, I thought to myself. I walked far- ther and didn't get very far until I saw a beam of light head for me. Quickly, I deflected it. I couldn't see much at all. I sent up a flare to light the sky. The sky lit up in a shade of blue, and I could see two holograms ahead. One of them waved its wand, and the trees started to move. One of the trees grabbed me with its branch and picked me up by my legs and turned me upside down. The two holograms fired multiple rays at me, and I shielded them off by enclosing a force field around me. Many times I fired back. I hit one hologram and then the next almost instantly and then cut myself down from the tree. I moved on, and the light from the flare died down and all I had to guide me was the glow of the wand. I walked on for an hour and had nothing else attack me; it was very quiet and very dark and scary.

"I must be close," I said out loud.

I had only walked a little farther when I stumbled upon a rocky pathway. It had become very dark, and I sent another flare up to see what was around me. The flare had lit the surroundings, and I could see a cave up ahead. I realised I was there. The warlock was somewhere inside the cave. I headed into the cave and made my wand burn brighter. I could not use flares inside the cave. It was dark and scary, and I thought to myself because fear was my vulnerability, he was using it to weaken me. I took a deep breath and moved on. I was tired, and it was cold. I never felt more vulnerable.

"Be brave, Bethany," I said to myself. I walked on farther in a narrow passageway until I stumbled into an opening. I stopped to take a rest. A few minutes later, the real warlock appeared. He fired a shot of some kind of ray, and it hit the camera. The light of the camera switched off, and I knew it was dead.

"What are you doing?" I screamed. He then cast a spell and a pink-coloured force field entrapped us both inside. I knew I couldn't breach the force field because it came from pink magic. I was trapped!

"It's time to test your power," exclaimed the warlock. "We will fight to the death!"

"Why are you doing this to me?" I cried.

"There was a prophecy that a witch will rule the kingdom. The prophecy predicted that he or she will be close to Zelda. I thought it would be a child of hers, so I stopped her from bearing a child. I later heard about you, and I can't have a human ruling the kingdom. I control the humans. I will lose control if the human become allies with the witches."

"You should not control anyone. I will stop you," I replied. "I would like to see you try!" he shouted, and then he fired a pink laser beam at me.

I covered a force field around me to prevent the beam from hitting me. It was only a temporary fix. The strong pink beam was weakening me.

"I need to find more strength," I said to myself. I thought back to what I learned in meditation then thought about the star. I closed my eyes and started meditating. It was difficult, but I managed to focus on the star. Slowly, I grew stronger and stronger. I meditated that I drew the energy from the star and focused on the energy running in my wand. All of a sudden, I felt my wand heat up. I then opened my eyes and fired a blue beam at the warlock. The power of the blue beam knocked the warlock of his feet, and I lifted the force field and fired a stun beam and knocked the warlock unconscious. I then trapped him in the blue force field.

I turned toward the camera and, with a spell, fixed the camera. "The warlock is trapped in the blue force field. It's over, it's over," I said in a puff.

CHAPTER 19

"Wake up, Bethany," said a concerned voice. I opened my eyes and saw Zelda sitting on the edge of the bed. "You were screaming. You had a nightmare, my dear." "Yes, um, maybe," I replied. "I dreamt about a warlock," I said. "No surprise. He tried to kill you," said Zelda. "No. It's a different warlock," I explained. "Oh?"

"Yes. A different warlock came to me in a dream and wanted to challenge me."

"To rule the kingdom?" questioned Zelda.

"No. He wanted to rule the world. He was young with peculiarly big eyes."

"It was just a dream," Zelda tried to reassure me. "It felt so real," I responded.

"Put it out of your mind because today is your day to meet the king."

"Yes, and after, I go back to Sandsdale."

"Yes!" Zelda replied. "You will reunite with your mother and your friends."

"Oh, Zelda. I'm excited!"

An hour passed and Zanda was waiting in a horse-drawn cart. "Come on, Bethany. Zanda is waiting for you," cried Zelda.

I rushed down to meet Zanda, forgetting about my breakfast. I was excited and was ready to meet the king. I entered the cart and gave Zanda a big kiss.

"You look pretty," said Zanda, looking at my dress that I save for special occasions.

"Thank you."

We rode to the school grounds where the king awaits. "The king will give a speech and then he will have his horse-drawn cart take you back to Sandsdale."

We pulled up behind the stage where the king was speaking to a large audience of witches. He gave an apology to the people for the wrongs that he'd done, and he promised a better future from now on. He said he wanted a better relationship with humans and witches, and he wanted for all of us to live together in harmony. He then spoke about me and was very excited to have me on his council and then he introduced me onto the stage. "Congratulations, Bethany," he said.

"Thank you," I replied.

"So tell me, Bethany, what are the first things you want to see change?" the king asked.

"The first thing is goodwill to men and witches. The second thing is to keep a promise."

"Oh? What do you mean?" questioned the king. "Well in order to become a powerful witch, I had to go through challenges. I came across many wrongs that I promised to make right. My first adventure was in the marshlands where I met trolls. In the marshlands, most of the animals have disappeared because of the warlock. I wish to have the animals returned, but I had to defeat the warlock first. Second was in the forest where the red phoenix lives. There was great destruction of their habitat. Trees were cut down and eggs were being taken. I wish to preserve the trees and keep safe the phoenix eggs. Third was in the lake where the giant oyster lives. The water was polluted so I cleaned it up. I wish for the lake to be kept clean. These are the promises I made, and I wish to keep them."

"And so it will be done," replied the king. "I want to give you this medallion for your bravery." The king took a small golden medallion with a pin on it and pinned it on my shirt. "This represents courage and bravery."

"Thank you, Your Majesty," I replied.

"Now for a surprise. I have plans to unite all the kingdoms of the north together. Bethany, I want you to come with me for nine months to the north and meet with all the kings."

My heart sank. I wanted just to go home. "When do I leave?"

I asked.

"In two days' time," he replied.

My heart sank further, but I felt it was necessary. "Okay, I will come. Can my fiance come with me?"

"Yes, he can," the king replied. "Thank you," I said.

"Okay, that is settled. The king's council horse and carriage await for you to take you back to Sandsdale."

I thanked the king and everyone. After that, I met Zelda and Zanda in the back of the stage. "Thank you, Zelda, for everything." I gave her a big hug.

"Go make a difference," she replied. "I will."

"Take good care of Zanda," she said.

"It's going to be over a year, but I will pay you a visit as soon as I can."

"Okay," she said, "you better get going."

I gave her another hug, and Zanda and I hopped in the cart and we rode off.

CHAPTER 20

We arrived at Sandsdale at 6:00 p.m. We stopped outside of Mum's house.
"Mum, I'm home!" I yelled. I ran to the house and opened the door. "Mum!" I cried.
"Bethany, is that you?" Mum replied.
"Yes." She walked out of the kitchen and gave me a big hug. "I have a lot to tell you, Mum."
"Yes. I heard from the king's newsman."
"I wanted to tell you I've fallen in love," I said. "Oh? With a witch?" she replied.
"Yes. I am engaged."
She gave a meaningful smile. "Congratulations!" she said. "Really? Are you proud of me?"
"Of course, Bethany. I am always proud of you, and everyone at Sandsdale is too."
"Thanks, Mum," I said and gave her a big hug.

Zanda came in and I introduced him to my mother, and we both spoke about our love for each other. We talked until late at night. I told her that I had to leave again to head north for nine months. She was sad but understood the importance of it.

The next day, I showed Zanda around Sandsdale, and he met everyone including Tom and Peter. Tom was so thrilled about my victory. Mum cooked us a big roast chicken. I enjoyed eating meat again, but Zanda just ate salad and potatoes. After lunch, I packed for my trip away. The next day, a cart was waiting at 5:00 a.m. Zanda and I hopped in the cart, and we rode off to the north. We rode on and on and stopped off for a rest and looked around small villages along the way.

On the fifth day, we arrived at the palace of one of the kingdoms of the north. I met up with the king inside the palace lounge. The king greeted me and instructed me to go out to the grounds out the back where many of king's junior council staff were. The king said he wanted to talk trade deals with the king and queen of the kingdom. I went out the back and met around ten ladies and gentleman of the local staff. I also noticed that there were two warlocks there. I stared closely at the warlocks hoping I would see one that was in my dream, but none of them were young and did not possess those big eyes that I would never forget.

Months rolled on by, and I had visited four kingdoms of the north. I met kings, queens, dukes, bishops, local men and women, witches, elves, and warlocks. I went to meeting after meeting but stayed mostly in the background, which was fine for me. After nine months, Zanda and I rode back to Sandsdale. Zanda and I settled in straight way. I worked most of the time either picking the berries off the wild bushes or milking the cows. Zanda was happy working on the tractor. No magic was used to help the farm along, just hard work. On the weekends, Zanda and I went up the hills for picnics. A month rolled on by and I was missing all the witches, especially Zelda. I decided to write to Zelda saying that I missed her, and I will pay her a visit soon. She wrote back to me two weeks later saying thing were alright here at the witches' village and she missed me too. At the end of the letter, she said she had news that she wanted to tell me but not to rush back for it wasn't urgent.

CHAPTER 21

I gave a gentle knock on Zelda's door. It didn't matter if I knocked hard or not because with a witches' door, you can hear the knock from all corners of the house. The door opened with Zelda on the other side.

"Hey!" I shrieked.

"Come in, Bethany." I walked into the house and the place looked particularly spotless.

"Have you been doing the spring cleaning?" I said. "Something like that," she replied.

"How have you been?" I said. "I've been keeping busy." "Oh?" I said curiously.

"I've been learning how to knit, and I've been knitting lots of garments."

"Really? That's great. I must see what you've done," I said. "In a minute. So how are you?" "Exhausted," I replied. "You must tell me of your adventures to the northern lands," she asked.

"Well, I travelled and travelled. I saw everything, but I was just in the background while the king mainly negotiated trade deals." I gave a sigh. "I don't feel like I belong on the king's council."

"It takes time to adjust, and change is slow. The king has his autonomy and that's what's most important," she explained, and I felt better.

"Enough about me. What is the news you wanted to share with me?"

"Patience," she said. "Let me show you what I've been knitting." She walked to the linen cupboard and took out some knitted clothing. I looked closer and noticed they were all baby's clothes.

"They are all baby's clothes," I said and remembered about the spell. That's right, the spell on Zelda not being able to bear a child would have been lifted ever since I beat the warlock. "Are you thinking of having a relationship and having a family?" I asked.

"Not quiet. Bethany, I had a child," she said. "What!?" I gasped.

"Yes. I got pregnant the day you left, and I had a baby boy," she said. I was confused.

"But how?"

"The condition of the spell. When the spell lifts, I will have a baby warlock."

My heart pounded. "You mean to say you're having the warlock's child?" I said loudly.

"Shh..." she whispered. "Something like that. It's my child, and I 'm going to raise it on my own."

I thought for a moment to take it all in. "You're not alone. You have Zanda and me to help." I suddenly heard crying from upstairs.

"Oh, he needs me." We both ran upstairs into my old room. Zelda raced to a large cot in the middle of the room and picked up the baby and cradled him over his shoulders.

"What's his name? Does he have one?" "Brendon."

"That's a beautiful name."

Zelda rocked the baby until he stopped crying. "Take him," she said.

"Really?" I said with glee. I took the baby and held him in my arms. I looked at his face and went pale. His eyes. I remember those big grey eyes. It was the warlock who was in my dreams.

"You look flushed, Bethany. Is everything alright?"

"Yes, fine. It's been an eventful day. Please take him." I handed Brandon back to Zelda. "I must go," I said.

"What, already?"

"Yes. I need to get back to Sandsdale." "Okay. I'll see you to the cart."

"I'll come back soon, and we will have a proper catch up," I said.

"Okay, my darling. You have a good journey back."

I gave her a last farewell and hopped in the cart. As the horse pulling the cart moved on, I waved goodbye at her. As we rode on, I thought about the child.

It was only a dream, I thought to myself.

As we moved forward, I looked back at Zelda's house and noticed a grey halo around her house. My heart began to pound. I learned about dark omens at school, and this was one of them.

It was a sign alright. A sign for dark times ahead.

www.ingramcontent.com/pod-product-compliance
Lightning Source LLC
LaVergne TN
LVHW060219080526
838202LV00052B/4306